Camping Stories

For kids

Kendall Lies His Way into Camping

Kendall was a seventh grader who loved to play a lot. While his younger sister, nine-year-old Kelly was reading, Kendall chose to play video games instead. Before he started seventh grade, Kendall was a good student who knew how to balance it all.

He knew when to play and he knew when to study. But when he started seventh grade, he borrowed a new video game from his friend and since then, all he ever did was play the game. He was now too lazy to study. When he was not playing the video game,

he chose to play out on the street rather than study.

"Kendall, have you finished reading?" His mother would ask him whenever she saw him playing games. And Kendall's usual reply was, "Yes, mom."

And this reply was always a lie. He never took out time to study. All Kendall ever wanted to do was play out in the yard or in the street, or in his room inside the house. His parents had not yet seen his grades for the new class so they believed Kendall whenever he told them he was studying. His parents were very sure that Kendall would do well in seventh grade just like he had done in previous classes.

Since Kendall did not like to study, it was no surprise that when it was time for his mid-term test, Kendall was not sure where to start studying from. He stared hard at the many pages of school books he had to read but Kendall did not know where to begin.

The boy was confused. Kendall shrugged and decided that he would not bother about the test. He would read the little he could and guess the answers he did not know, Kendall told himself. The boy felt very proud of his decision and now that his mind was made up, he headed back to his games. He was going to spend all of the summer having a blast outside! He could hardly wait.

Well... Kendall's dreams of a fun summer holiday were dashed that evening during dinner.

"Guess what we will be doing at the start of your summer holiday," his father asked while they were eating.

Excited, Kendall looked up and squealed, "What? What is it, dad? What are we going to be doing?"

"Well, you know how you both have wanted to go camping for a long time? Well, we will be doing so," his father announced.

Kendall and Kelly jumped up and down in excitement. They loved camping but they did not go as often as they wanted to because their parents were always busy with work. It was no surprise that they were this excited at the opportunity to go camping.

"When are we leaving, dad? Immediately the holiday starts? How long are we going to be out there?" a very excited Kelly asked.

Their mother laughed and said, "Slow down, Kelly. One at a time, for your dad and I will answer all your questions."

"Well, tell us already!" Kendall grinned.

"Well, we will be leaving the Friday after school closes for the break. We will be spending the weekend in the great outdoors. But, remember that you have to do well in your tests."

"What?" Kendall's mouth fell open. He looked from his father to his mother, and back to his father, "What happened to our tests?"

"Your tests, son. The camping trip is a reward for all your hard work this term. If you don't work hard and do well, you don't get rewarded," his father said with a shrug.

Kendall swallowed hard as he said, "So.. so... we have to ace our tests?"

"Exactly," his mother smiled. "But I'm sure that won't be a problem for you both. My two babies study so well. This is just additional incentive."

"I for one, I'm excited about this reward, mom, dad. It's pumped me up and I can't wait to ace my tests!" Kelly cheered.

"Kendall, why aren't you saying anything? Aren't you confident that you'll do well in your tests?" his father asked him.

Kendall faked a smile and nodded slowly, "Sure, I'm sure I will do well too, mom, dad."

"That's a good boy," his father smiled and Kendall smiled but inside his head, he was crying. The little boy did not want to miss the camping trip but he was confused because he did not know what to do. He looked at his father and said, "So, dad, do you mean that if one of us does not do well in the test, that person will stay back home while the rest of you go camping?"

Kendall was thinking to himself that that was not so bad. If that was the case, his parents would probably take him to his grandparents. Being with

his grandparents was always fun and it was also a reward. It would be a bigger reward because it would be just him there and they would definitely dote on him so much. A smile started to form on his lips but his father's next words cut it off.

"Of course not, son. If anyone of you fails the test, the camping trip is canceled and it's just going to be a summer break at home." his father smiled and patted their hands, "I have no doubt that the camping trip will be a success because my children are such good students and you always do okay."

"Yeah, right?" Kendall nodded, now his internal tears had resumed. What was he going to do? If he failed, not only would he not be able to go for the trip, but the others wouldn't too. His sister was going to be very angry at him if they missed the trip because of him. Kendall turned to his sister and saw her smiling at their parents. She was probably not in his situation. The smile on her face said that she had been studying a lot and she was probably confident that she would ace the test.

Oh no! What will I do? Kendall asked himself once more.

*

"Old man Donald had a farm, e-i-e-i-o, and on his farm he had some cows, e-i-e-i-o, with a moo-moo there, and a moo-moo here, everywhere a moo-moo..." Kelly sang at the top of her lungs as the car drove down the dirt road into the park. Usually, Kendall would sing along with her but he could not do it this time around. He was not enjoying the ride one bit. He had told a huge lie and it was affecting him a lot. He had failed his test but he had lied to his parents that he passed and now, they were on their way to have a fun camping weekend. But all Kendall could think about was the fact that he had told a huge lie.

They drove into the clearing where they would be setting up their camp and they all alighted the car. The family got to work setting up their tents. Once the tents were set and the car had been unpacked, Kelly and their dad left so they could gather wood for their campfire. Kendall was left with his mother to set out the marshmallows and prepare hot cocoa.

"Are you okay, Kendall?" his mother asked him many times and every time, the boy told her that he was well, even though he knew that he was telling more lies.

It was evening when Kelly and daddy returned so they built the fire and they sat around it, laughing and nursing mugs of hot cocoa.

"This is fun," their father said. "The air is cool and the company is nice."

"Tell us a story, dad!" Kelly said excitedly.

"Does everyone want a story?" their father laughed and they all nodded happily, everyone but Kendall.

"Okay, I will tell you a fun story then. I hope you enjoy it," their father said as he winked.

"My story is about a boy called Ollie. Ollie lived outside the village and he took care of lots of sheep. Many of the villagers bought sheep from Ollie because his prices were nice and many people in the village liked him. You see, Ollie lived alone. Ollie's house was surrounded by a fence, and the fence was surrounded by trees.

Ollie played with the children of the village sometimes and other times, he played by himself in his house, when he was not selling his sheep. One day, Ollie was bored and he decided to play a prank on the people in the village. He ran into the village and cried that wolves were attacking his sheep."

"Oh no!" Kelly exclaimed.

"Oh yes!" their father nodded and he continued the story.

"All the villagers gathered their cutlasses and they followed Ollie to drive away the wolves that were disturbing his sheep. The villagers left behind all they had been doing to help Ollie. Some were cooking, some were washing, some were playing, some were reading, some were farming, but they all left it behind as they wanted to help Ollie.

But when the villagers got to Ollie's house, they saw his sheep grazing in the fields peacefully.

There were no wolves attacking them and Ollie laughed and told the villagers that he had played a prank on them. Of course the villagers were angry at Ollie. They had all left their stuff behind because of his lie. But instead of being sorry, Ollie kept laughing at the villagers' shocked faces, angering them. The angry villagers returned to their homes.

Two days later, Ollie's sheep were really under attack from wolves and he ran to ask for help from the villagers. No one believed him and they refused to follow him. Ollie returned to his farm alone and all his sheep were killed by the wolves. Ollie had no more sheep to sell and he became a poor, sad boy. And he learned how important the truth is and how wrong it is to lie. His lie made him to lose the villagers' trust and they refused to

believe him when he was telling the truth. Sadly, he learned his lesson the hard way. Let us not tell lies so we won't be like Ollie."

"Wow, that's a sad story. Ollie lost all he had because he chose to lie. He lost the villagers' trust because of his lie. And they could not help him when he needed them," Kelly said sadly.

"Exactly. That is what lies do, they make people to lose trust in you," their father said.

"Hey, I just remembered a song I learned in school. Just like daddy's story, it teaches us about lying!" an excited Kelly said.

"Why don't you teach us the song so we can sing it together, Kelly?" their mother asked.

"It goes like this," Kelly said, and she began:

Just as a river flows, so does a lie,

It keeps going, on and on,

It never stops, it never ends,

Where one lie ends, there another lie begins,

The cycle of lies is winding,

When you say one lie,

You have to say yet another,

Liar, liar, liar, it's not a good name

Stay away from lies,

They are nothing but trouble...

For where a lie ends, another lie begins...

When you say a lie,

No one will trust you...

Stay away from lies, they're nothing but trouble...

Kendall adjusted on the stone he was seated on as his parents and his sister sang the song over and over. It had a catchy tune and they were having lots of fun. But Kendall was having no fun. He felt as if the song was talking to him, even though he knew that no one knew about his lie.

"That is a really good song, Kelly. It certainly teaches how wrong lying is, just like the story," their mother said.

"That is true," their father agreed, "When you tell one lie, you always have to tell another to cover that one up and the cycle continues. it's really

not good to tell lies. When you tell lies, you will be seen as a liar, and no one will trust you."

Kendall could not take it anymore and he cried, "I lied! I lied that I passed my test because I wanted to come camping but I really didn't. I haven't been reading well and so, I didn't do well. I'm sorry, mom, dad, Kelly. I just didn't want us to lose out on the fun because of my laziness."

His mother sighed and hugged him. "That's why you've been so sad?"

"Yes!" he cried. "I know now that lies are bad, please forgive me and trust me once more."

His father patted his back, "That's okay, son. I am glad you did the right thing and told us the truth. But you know that you will be punished when we return home, right?"

"I deserve it."

Kendall cried and his family hugged him. The family sat around the fire telling more stories for the rest of the night. From that day on, Kendall never told a lie as he now knew how wrong it was to tell a lie.

A Cub Joins the Camping Trip

The wind was very strong in the woods. It blew so very hard and shook the tree branches. Fruits fell like the rain from the trees. The monkeys ran to the bananas and they munched on them quickly. The squirrels ran to the acorns and they ate them up as quickly as they could.

The bears were having a feast with the berries that graced the forest floor. None of the animals in the woods had to stress themselves to feed that afternoon because the strong wind was helping them out a great deal.

"It looks like rain," Grandma Bear said as she looked up to the sky. The clouds were gathering and the sky was already darkening. Night had not fallen yet so the darkness was not due to the sun's disappearance. Grandma Bear looked around and saw that her grand-bear cubs were complete. Sternly, grandma bear said to the ten cubs. "Do not leave the den, cubs. The wind out there is too strong and if you go out there, you can get lost. So, stay close to me."

"What of mama and papa?' the youngest of the cubs, Jimmy cried. "They are trapped out there. We have to help them."

"Don't you worry about a thing, Jimmy. Your parents can take care of themselves. They know these woods even with their eyes closed. You all just worry about yourselves and do as I have instructed. Now, now, let's go in."

Reluctantly, Jimmy let his grandma lead him into the den. But when he got inside, Jimmy could not stay still. Though his grandma had said his parents would be able to find their way back home, the little cub was not convinced and he was greatly worried about them. As if to worsen his fears, thunder clapped through the sky just then, shaking the large tree where their den was. Jimmy headed to the exit but a voice stopped him, causing him to pause in his step.

"Don't even think about it, Jimmy. It's not going to end well."

Jimmy turned around and grinned sheepishly when he saw his oldest sister, Mirabel eyeing him from a perch in the tree. He forced a laugh as he scratched his hairy head.

"What are you talking about? I just wanted to see if the rain has started to fall. That's all," he quickly said but his sister's expression told him that she was not falling for his lie.

She stalked closer to him and said, "Listen to grandma and stay put. Mama and papa have survived several trips out in a storm even before you were born. I learned from experience that they can survive out there so I don't worry about them as much. You shouldn't either. And you certainly should not put yourself in harm's way. You know that that's the last thing they would want."

"What?? I'm not putting myself in harm's way. Just innocently checking out the weather, is all," Jimmy said quickly.

Mirabel patted his head as she said, "Tsk, I know you Jimmy. Whenever you start scratching

your head like that, you're obviously nervous. You can't deceive me, my dear little brother. Now go inside and play with our siblings."

"I hear you." Jimmy lowered his head and started heading farther into the tree. His sister called out to him and he turned to her.

She said, "If you try to leave again, I'll tell grandma to send the monkeys that live in the tree across from ours after you. You know how much they like to tickle. You are going to suffer a tickle-fest which I know you don't like."

Jimmy gulped and he nodded. He dreaded tickles and indeed, he had to give it to his sister for being smart enough to threaten him with that.

His head still lowered, Jimmy headed back to his siblings, deciding to obey his sister.

While he was trying to get into the game his siblings were playing, stronger lightning struck and thunder clapped repeatedly. The cub gritted his teeth as he tried hard not to let it bother him. He was amazed at how cool and collected his siblings were. He just could not see himself being that way.

Jimmy finally found his chance to flee when his grandma called them out to have lunch. The little cub felt he had to find his parents and help lead them back to the tree they called home. He was convinced that they had gotten lost. They were supposed to be home by now and the rain might just fall. If it fell, then they would definitely be trapped out there.

During the chaos of his siblings hurrying out of the room in the tree to meet his grandma, Jimmy took advantage and slipped out of a small opening in the back of the tree. As soon as he was on the outside, the bear tried jumping from one tree to the other. But before long, he was exhausted and he had

to slink to the forest floor and move around. He would find his parents, the bear thought to himself determinedly.

He turned around a bend and found himself smack in the middle of a cluster of trees. To his left, several had already fallen to the floor already, brought down by the wind. He hoped nobody had gotten hurt. Listening hard, he could not see anyone.

"Hurry up and find mama and papa," the bear said to himself. The sun would soon set and he was really getting worried.

He turned around and saw that there were trees behind him too. Jimmy ran forward but he was confused about which way to turn. He kept running around in circles but the cub could not find his way out to more familiar surroundings.

"Oh no! I think I am lost! Whatever am I going to do?" the cub wondered just as tears welled up in his eyes. He shook his head stubbornly. "I will not cry. I am not going to cry. I will find my parents and go home," he said in a weak voice.

He resumed trying to find his way out.

*

Misha licked her lips after she bit into the s'more. "It's so good," the girl exclaimed. "This will be perfect with hot cocoa."

"Coming right up," her big sister, Nora said as she brought out a thermos and filled their cups.

Helen, Misha's second oldest sister handed her another plate of s'mores and she did not waste time munching on it. Misha grinned and pulled closer to the fire. It was fun going camping with her sisters. It had been a long time they did an outdoor activity and the twelve-year-old was really enjoying this one.

Misha suddenly started singing:

I love my marshmallows, crackers and chocolate

It gives me my best camping treat... s'mores!

I tell you, hot cocoa and s'mores

Nothing beats the combined sweetness!

Next to the warm campfire

Toasting marshmallows and telling stories is the best!

Camping out in the woods,

Is never complete without s'mores!

Helen laughed at her sister's song.

"Did you just form that song because of s'mores?"

"No. I've been working on it for a long time," Misha grinned.

"I like it. It's catchy," Nora said as she sat next to them. "Teach me the song, Misha."

The two sisters continued to sing while Helen looked up at the sky. "The wind is still strong, girls. Are you sure it won't rain? I think we should head into the tent and zip up for the night."

"Please, please, pretty please, let's wait a little longer. The fire is so warm," Misha said as she stretched her hands over it.

"Yeah, just a little while longer, Helen. We are spending just one night here so we should try to make the most of it," Nora winked at her younger sister.

"Fine, fine," Helen agreed, causing Misha to clap in excitement.

Nora stepped away for a few minutes and she returned. She said to her sisters. "I think we should call it a night. The wind is still very strong and I could not see any other campers around here. We made a mistake to set up here. You know we are supposed to set up our tents where we can see other people."

"Well at least it's just one night, right?" Misha said. She pointed at the large tent the sisters had set earlier. "And we placed our tents away from trees so it's safe. If a tree falls, it won't fall on our tent."

"Yes, that was good of us. Next time, we shouldn't fail to recheck the weather forecast before leaving home," Helen added and they all nodded in agreement.

The sisters quenched the campfire. Then, they finally went into the tent and they zipped up the entrance. Their net was water-proof so even if rain fell, they would still be protected. The only problem would be the cold and the mud the next morning.

The rain started sometime around midnight and the sisters cuddled inside their sleeping bags, wrapped with thick blankets.

Pit-pat, pit-pat, plat-splash, plat-splash, the rain went, falling hard on their tent and everywhere around them.

And within the sound of the rain, there was another sound. It went thus: *Boohoo wah! Boohoo wah! Boohoo wah! Boohoo wah!*

When the rain let up a little and became just: *pit pit pit-splash, pit pit pit-splash,* the other sound became very obvious.

Misha woke up suddenly and she looked around in fear.

"What's that sound?" she whispered.

"I'm sure it's just the wind, Misha, go back to sleep," Helen said sleepily.

"No, no, it sounds like someone is crying. Listen," Misha whispered as she shook her sister awake.

A groaning Helen woke up, "Misha, no one is going to be awake and crying at this time of the night. Look, it's... where is my phone? See? It's one am. Sleep, will you?"

"What if it's a ghost?" Misha gasped.

"Oh no…" Helen groaned louder. All she wanted to do was sleep.

Nora sat up and grabbed a torch, "Come on, let's go check it out. When we see it's not a ghost and it's just the wind, maybe we'll all be able to get some sleep."

The sisters wore raincoats and crawled out of the tent. They zipped it behind them and headed in the direction of the sound, the torch illuminating their path. Misha gasped and she pointed to a small bush. Skulking and shaking like a wet leaf was a small bear cub. The cub was crying.

"It's a cub. It must have strayed away from his family!" she exclaimed as she ran towards it.

"What are you doing, Misha? You know bear cubs are not like teddy bears, right? They aren't harmless. Stay away from it!" Helen called to her.

"Well, we can't just leave it out here in the rain, can we?" Misha asked stubbornly. "Look at him. He's all wet. The rain is going to get heavier again and he'll be sick by morning."

Misha reached out to the shivering bear cub and she pulled off her rain coat and wrapped it around him. She looked at her sisters with puppy eyes and said, "He's too big for me to carry."

Sighing loudly, Nora stepped forward and carried the cub while Helen carried Misha and they ran back to their tent. They got in in time because the rain came down heavily again.

Misha wiped the cub with a towel till he was dry and no longer shivering.

"There, there, try to get some sleep."

"I wonder how he got away from his family," Helen said out loud.

"It's raining. Maybe he got lost. Anyway, we'll try to find them tomorrow before we leave. I don't think I'll be able to get any sleep tonight," Nora said, looking at her sister who was cuddling next to the bear.

The bear had stopped crying and he was now snug under the blanket. The tent was already stretched. But there was nothing the sisters could do but manage the situation.

Jimmy the cub's eyes kept darting around the tent. He was so glad to be out of the rain and cold. This was his fault. If only he had listened to his grandma, he would not have gotten lost. He had walked and walked and walked around but he had not been able to find his home or any other animal. He had strayed from their territory and then, darkness fell.

Jimmy had been so scared but then he had heard happy voices singing. He liked the song and he liked the delicious smell coming from their fire. But most of all, he had wanted to be next to the fire where it was warm.

Little Jimmy's happiness had disappeared when the three singing humans put off the fire and went into their small home. And so, he had curled up in a bush and cried as the rain fell. He was so glad they had found him. He wished he could tell them he was hungry but they could not understand him.

Jimmy's eyes lit up when Misha gave him some berries. He gobbled them up and now satisfied, he slept off. As he drifted away, he made a promise to himself. He would never disobey the older cubs again. He had gotten lost due to his disobedience. Never again would he be stubborn.

The next morning, the sisters walked farther into the woods with Jimmy and Jimmy ran off as he saw his family. He hugged them tightly and he promised to always behave. They had missed him a lot.

Smiling, the three sisters headed back to their tent. It had been a fun and unusual camping trip; one they would remember for a long time.

Tales by The Campfire

Three little girls ran out of their parents' car as soon as it stopped moving. They ran to a group of other little girls who were standing in a corner.

Vroom, vroom, more cars were stopping and out of the cars came little kids, all hugging their parents and running off to look for their friends.

"Hi! Hi! Hello! Hello!" The little ones called to each other.

"It's good to see you. I missed you!" Those were the words they said to their friends.

The parents stood a little way from the children. They watched their happy kids play with their friends.

"Hello! Hello!" came a voice in the distance. The parents turned to see who it was. It was Mrs. Big, the camp director!

"I am so happy to see you all. I'm glad you were able to bring your little ones to summer camp!" an excited Mrs. Big told the parents.

The parents clapped and thanked Mrs. Big for because of her, their kids would have a fun start of their summer break at camp!

"Is there anything we could do to help you out, Mrs. Big?" the parents asked the little woman.

"No, thank you. I promise you that your kids will have a fun weekend for we will have lots of games and activities!"

Mrs. Big was very different from her name. While her name was Big, she was small in size! And she had a head of gray hair. Mrs. Big was small in size but the same could not be said about her heart.

Mrs. Big had a large heart and she loved children! This was why she held the camp! So the children could play. The children could play as much as they wanted. They could have enough fun. And the children could make new friends! For the children came from different places all around.

Mrs. Big waved goodbye to the parents and then, she went to meet the children. They were all waiting for her. As soon as the children saw Mrs. Big, they hugged her. They hugged Mrs. Big because they had missed her. The children loved Mrs. Big and her camp. Last summer, they had all been at her camp. It had been a very fun experience. And this year, there were more kids. Everyone had heard

about Mrs. Big's two-day summer camp. They were all eager to check it out. When it was not summer, all the children looked forward to Mrs. Big's camp. They always tried to behave themselves because the perfect punishment a parent could give was to prevent a child from attending Mrs. Big's fun camp.

No child wanted to miss the camp, so they ensured to always be on their best behavior! So again, the parents had Mrs. Big to thank for their kids' obedience, for she created the fun camp that no kid wanted to miss.

There was always a lot to do at Mrs. Big's camp. No child got bored at the fun camp. Games,

sports, campfire nights, they were part of what made life so great at Mrs. Big's camp.

"Mrs. Big, we missed you so much!" they cried. "It is so good to see you again. Did you miss us as much as we missed you?"

"Of course I did, you don't have to ask. For I kept looking forward to the summer so I can see all your pretty little faces again. And look, we have some new children with us. Isn't it nice that we get to make more friends? Friendship is such a beautiful thing and I am happy that we get to share it with more children."

"We can't wait to get started too, Mrs. Big!" the happy children said together.

The children followed Mrs. Big as she led them to the area where tents had been arranged for them to sleep.

When it's time to sleep, what do we do?

We turn off the lights and we turn in for the night!

Sleep time is time to say goodbye to the world,

Nighttime is time to say goodbye to our friends

Lala land is where we go when we say good night,

Lala land is where we go when we turn off the lights and sleep!

The children sang together as Mrs. Big showed them their sleeping bags. From the tents, Mrs. Big led the children to the kitchen area and they broke into another song:

If you want to grow, you should eat your food

Food is good for children, to make us grow...

Mealtime shouldn't be avoided

It's time to sit and eat

Try to eat all the food on your plate

Don't skip any, not even the veggies.

Eat all your food so you can grow!

Healthy and strong!

They moved through all the parts of the camp, singing and having fun. The newcomers easily

caught on and learned the songs. The children had learned the songs their first time at Mrs. Big's fun camp. Mrs. Big's fun camp was a two-day fun-filled activity that always left the children feeling happy and anticipating the next time. Mrs. Big was like their bubbly grandmother who loved and cared for them and told them stories. Oh! The children loved her stories. No one could tell stories as good as Mrs. Big. She was the best storyteller in the world to the kids.

"Mrs. Big? When are we going to have story time?" one of the children asked her, tugging on her shawl.

"Soon, my dear Emma. We will have our story time during our campfire later in the night."

"Woo hoo! Story time! Campfire!! Marshmallows!!" the children shouted in happiness. Story time while enjoying a campfire and toasting marshmallows was the best way to spend a night in camp! All the children agreed on this.

"Well, kids, time to have your shower, then we will have story time. Who is in?"

"Me! Me! Me!" the children cried at the same time.

"Perfect! Let's get to the showers!" Mrs. Big cheered and the laughing children ran as fast as their legs could carry them to the showers. No one wanted to be late for story time.

*

Clean and fed, the children were gathered around Mrs. Big by the campfire. Mrs. Big's friends were assisting the children as they toasted the marshmallows so they would not hurt themselves.

"Mrs. Big? Please tell us a story. You always have such fun stories," one of the children said and the others nodded.

"Yes, Mrs. Big, do tell us a story..."

Mrs. Big's friends nodded in agreement and they said along with the children, "Tell us a story, Mrs. Big. The campfire can never be complete without your amazing stories."

Mrs. Big smiled brightly and she looked into the fire, "Of course, my little ones. I will tell you a story. I have a nice story to tell. I hope you like it."

Mrs. Big winked and the children laughed. She began her first story:

"Long ago, in a small village near the sea, there lived a little boy and his name was Humpty.

Humpty loved to play by the seaside, and he loved to gather seashells. But most of all, Humpty loved to sing. Humpty could sing for hours and he never got tired. Humpty was also very proud and he loved going around the village, singing at the top of his lungs.

Humpty never got tired of singing but sometimes, his voice became hoarse. And so, his mother always told him to take it easy. 'You are not competing with anyone, Humpty dear. You have to be careful so you won't lose your voice,' she always said to Humpty. But Humpty never listened to his mother. He continued to sing, and sing and sing. In the morning, he sang. In the afternoon while he was

gathering shells, he sang and in the nights when everyone was fast asleep, Humpty kept singing.

The villagers went to meet Humpty's mother and they said, 'We know that Humpty has a good voice and we all enjoy it but he sings too much. Can he please stop singing in the nights? We all try to get some sleep then and Humpty singing always is of no help to us. He can sing as much as he wants in the day but he should please leave the night for us. Humpty's mother, Mrs. Dumpty was about to speak when Humpty ran out of his room and he glared at the villagers. Humpty shouted, 'No! I won't stop singing. All of you are jealous of my voice and I won't let you have it!'

'Please Humpty, all we want to do is sleep. You can sing at any other time of the day but the night. Let us sleep well,' the villagers pleaded with Humpty.

'No!' Humpty refused stubbornly. 'My voice travels very far in the night. I won't stop singing in the night just because you beg me to stop. You have to live with it.'

After the villagers left, Humpty's mother pleaded with him some more but Humpty refused to listen to her. His mind was made up."

"So what happened next, Mrs. Big? Did the villagers continue to have sleepless nights?" one of the children asked.

"Oh those poor villagers. Why didn't Humpty pity them and sing just in the daytime?" another child spoke up.

"The story is not yet finished, my little ones. Listen some more:

Humpty discovered dancing and he realized that he was a good dancer and so, Humpty started dancing together with singing. Just like with singing, Humpty practiced until late in the night. He danced

so loudly that everyone around him could hear his footfalls. He danced and sang, danced and sang, continuously disturbing the villagers. But there was nothing the villagers could do. Humpty never listened to them. He was arrogant and refused to mingle with them or hear what they had to say. The villagers had to manage with their sleepless night.

The king of the kingdom held a contest and he called for artistes from far and wide. The winner was going to win a thousand gold coins. But that was not the only prize, the winner would also become the palace's performer, a position that meant more gold coins! When Humpty heard about the contest, he

was excited. He knew he was the best and he was sure he was going to win. There was no doubt.

And so, his practice became worse and more frequent. 'Humpty, my son. Why don't you calm down and think of the people as well as yourself? If you continue at this rate, you are bound to hurt yourself. You will be tired by the day of the contest. Remember that you are also hurting the people,' his mother pleaded with him again.

'I am king and I am the best. I can do whatever I want. I never get tired,' came Humpty's reply.

His mother always sighed and returned to her room. There was no talking to Humpty. He was proud and stubborn.

The day of the contest arrived and the previous night, Humpty had as usual, kept his neighbors up with his practice.

'If Humpty wins, he will move into the palace and we will finally be free from his singing and dancing,' one of his neighbors said that morning.

'Yes! Yes! I really do hope he wins. Our freedom will only come if Humpty wins. We have to go there and cheer him up. Seeing supporters will

inspire him and help him do his very best. Then, we will be free!'

The palace was filled with lots of people from far and wide. Everyone wanted to see who the great king would reward. A very confident Humpty arrived at the palace feeling very sure if himself. He saw many contestants but he was not bothered. He knew he was the best so there was nothing for him to worry about. He bounced in feeling on top of the world and ready to win."

"Did he win, Mrs. Big?" the children asked impatiently.

"Patience little ones, exercise patience. In due time, all your questions will be answered."

The children were staring at Mrs. Big in awe, very much eager to know what would be the end for Humpty. Would he finally leave the village alone or would he lose and return to the village? They all wondered.

"Many contestants sang before it was Humpty's turn and they were all really good but Humpty was still not bothered. He knew he was winning it. Finally, it was his turn and he was called up to the stage.

'Humpty Dumpty!!' the announcer called.

Cheers broke out across the room, most of them from his neighbors. They were going to be super happy to see him leave the neighborhood.

Humpty started singing and he broke into a dance as he sang. His voice was very melodious and the entire courtyard broke out in cheers. He was loved by all and the king even started dancing. His dance steps were perfect and before long, everyone was dancing along with Humpty. Humpty was not done showcasing his talent. He made a leap onto the palace walls which surrounded the courtyard and continued dancing. But then suddenly, Humpty fell

fatigue wash over him. All the fatigue from the previous day, the past week, the past months, they all rushed into him and Humpty lost his balance. He felt himself falling off the wall and there was nothing he could do to stop it. He screamed but no one could get to him on time. Humpty hit the ground, splat, and he was gone!"

"Oh no!" the children gasped. "Why did Humpty have to be so stubborn? He should have learned to rest and stopped being proud and a pest! Poor Humpty!"

"Exactly! Humpty should have listened to everyone! And so, the villagers started singing a

song in remembrance of Humpty and whenever they heard the song, it was a reminder to them that they should stop whatever they were doing and rest because while working hard is important, so also is creating the time to rest!" Mrs. Big said to them. And she began to sing:

Humpty Dumpty sat on the wall,

Humpty Dumpty had a great fall,

All the king's horses, and all the king's men,

Couldn't put Humpty together again!

"So, was that the end of Humpty, Mrs. Big?"

"Oh no, children. There's more. We already know that Humpty never took a break, right? Well, when he became a ghost, he didn't rest either! Humpty kept dancing and singing around the palace every single night! The king's family would wake up and see his ghost dancing, they would hear him singing too! And it is said that sometimes, he went out into the village and whenever he saw anyone sleeping, he would dance and sing and wake them up. Since he never slept, he refused to let anyone else sleep! He was the ghost who drove sleep far, far away!"

"Arghh!!!!" the children screamed.

Mrs. Big laughed and she clapped her hands. "Time to go to sleep, children. Tomorrow, we will resume our story time. And I promise that Humpty won't find you when you sleep!"

Still screaming, the children ran towards their tents. Chuckling, Mrs. Big and her friends headed after them to sing them goodnight.

The Ultimate Camping Toolkit

The sun was shining outside

The wind was blowing softly.

It was a warm and happy summer.

On the street, kids were playing and enjoying the break.

Some were on bikes,

Some were skipping,

Some were skating,

The street was filled with their laughter as they all had fun.

Up above in the trees, the birds sang,

Tweet, tweet, chirpity chirp, went the birds.

Down the corner, the dogs played with their little owners,

Arf, arf, woof, woof.

The kids tossed around with their kittens,

Meow, meow, purr, purr, went the kittens.

All the children were happy,

They were glad for the summer.

There was a white house down the street.

It had a red door and white windows.

There were bright red flowers in the front
yard,

And there were apple trees in the back yard.

A little girl called Nina lived in this house.

She lived with her mother, her father and her brother, Carlos.

Nina was twelve years old and her brother was ten years old.

Nina was very excited for this summer. She was happier than she had been in a long time. Why? It was because this summer, she was going to go camping with her family.

Nina had never ever gone camping, but her friends had gone camping.

Nina's friends always told great stories about their camping trips. They always sounded like

fun. So, Nina was very eager to experience the fun that her friends always talked about. When her parents told her they would be going camping for the weekend, she had squealed at the top of her lungs.

She could hardly wait. Their first camping trip ever! She planned to have as much fun as she could! She would be able to tell her friends all about her trip too!

"Are you ready, Nina?" her mother called up to her.

The little girl who had been at her room window, watching the kids playing outside ran to meet her mother. They were going shopping. Since it was their first time camping, they did not have any camping equipment. So, they were all going out to buy what they needed to go camping.

Nina's father and mother were in the front of the car while she sat in the back with her brother.

Going to the mall,

We're going to the mall,

We're going to the mall to get what we need.

It's fun at the mall,

We'll have fun at the mall,

There are so many things to see.

Food to eat, things to buy,

The mall is a very fun place.

We're going to the mall,

We're going to the mall, to buy what we need!

Nina sang. Her brother started the next verse while she clapped her hands and hummed along.

When we get to the mall,

We shouldn't run away,

We should always stick to our parents.

It's easy to get lost at the mall,

So we shouldn't go off by ourselves.

We're going to the mall,

We're going to the mall,

We're going to have fun at the mall!

We're going to the mall, to buy what we need!

We're going to the mall!

When they arrived at the mall, Nina went with her mother while her brother went with her father. They were headed to get all the food and kitchen equipment they would need for their camping trip. Nina and her mother walked into a large shop and her eyes went big when she saw so many colorful objects around her. Her mother took a trolley and together, they walked down an aisle.

Her mother said, "When we go camping, Nina, there are lots of things we need to have, and it's good that we don't forget any of them. Some of them are essential, that means they are very important. We have to have them. And others are not essential but it would be nice if we have them. But, we can still survive without them. Do you know any essential camping equipment?"

Nina thought about it for a short while and then, an idea popped into her head. "I know! I know! A tent! My friends always talk about tents! We need a tent. Right, mummy?"

"Yes, dear girl. Indeed we need a tent. And that's just one of many things we need to buy. Come along with me and let's go around the shop, buying all that we need for our first family camping trip! I'll show you all we need to have a good camping trip."

Camping takes us to nature,

We are away from our homes,

We are away from our beds,

We will be out in nature so there are some things we need to get...

"How do we shield ourselves from rain, mum?"

That's what a tent is for.

The tent protects us from the sun and rain.

It protects us from the cold

The tent is our little home away from home,

It serves as our shelter when we are camping.

We need the footprint and stakes as well,

For they'll serve to keep our tent in place.

"Okay, so if the tent is our roof, where do we sleep, mum? On the earth inside the tent?"

A sleeping bag is what we need, when we go

camping!

It serves as our bed and it's very soft,

We don't need to sleep on the earth!

A sleeping bag is well-padded and so we're

protected from the cold!

"Ah, I see mummy. So now, we have our tents and sleeping bags. What else do we need? What are we going to sit on at the camp? Surely, not the floor."

No, my dear girl, we have camp chairs for that...

When we want to sit at camp, we use our camp chairs...

See?

They are foldable so we can carry them everywhere we go!

A camp table is not an essential...

For we don't know if our camp will have one!

But it's best for us to get it, just in case!

"I'm a little scared, mom. Since there won't be electricity out there, how are we going to see?"

Light will always find us, that is not a problem.

Once we have all we need, we'll be able to see brightly!

We just need a lantern, flashlights, fuel and batteries.

Once we have all those, we are completely covered.

There is no way we can stay in the dark.

Worry not, my dear girl.

There's no reason to be scared.

We won't let you stay in the dark for we'll even build a campfire.

"That's nice, mama. I can't wait!"

The next day, the family filled their truck with the camping equipment and headed up the hill to a park close by. It was warm and nice and there were other families near them.

"How do we set up the net, daddy?" Carlos asked.

"Oh I'll show you both. Here we go."

This is the way we set up a tent, set up a tent, set up a tent...

This is the way we set up a tent, when we go camping...

First, we lay the tarp on the grass, on the grass, on the grass, first of all we lay the tarp so our sleeping bags won't get wet...

Next, we place the tent on the tarp, on the tarp, on the tarp... Next, we place the tent on the tarp, on the tarp...

After that, we connect the poles, connect the poles, connect the poles...

After that we connect the poles so we can start setting up the net...

Then we insert the poles inside the tent flaps, inside the tent flaps, inside the tent flaps... We insert the poles inside the tent flaps... so the tent can stand...

Now, we raise the tent, raise the tent, raise the tent...

Now, we raise the rent! We are almost done!

The last thing to do is stake the tent to the ground, to the ground. Now, we stake the tent, so it will be firm.

Yes, the tent is ready... The tent is ready... The tent is ready... Yes... The tent is ready, we are ready to camp!

The children clapped when they saw the finished tent. They were all done.

"Let's gather wood so we can build the fire!" Their mother said and they all hurried away with her.

The family set stones around a circle and then, placed small leaves at the center. They used matches to light up the leaves. They placed the larger wood and smaller sticks near the small leaves and slowly, the fire spread. Their father waved at the flames so that it could get stronger.

"Wow! We made a campfire!" the children cheered.

"Yeah, we did."

"This camping trip is going to be one of the best ever!" Nina exclaimed and her family laughed.

The Campfire Is Not the Only Fun Thing to Do at Camp

It was a bright summer afternoon and everyone out on the tree-lined street were bright. Though the day outside was bright, the five children in the house next to the orange tree were not bright. They had frowns on their faces.

Anna, Becca, Chad, Devon and Elisa were the five children. Anna was the oldest and Elisa was the youngest.

Their parents kept looking at them and wondering what the problem was.

"Why the frowns, kids? It is a beautiful day, unlike yesterday. Did you not hear what your father and I just announced? We are going camping! You should be happy!" Their mother said.

"Why should we be happy when we are not going to have fun over there?" Devon asked and the other four nodded in agreement.

"What are you talking about, children? Camping is always fun!"

"No, it's never fun. All we ever do when we go camping is sit by the fire. It would be fun if we actually had story hour or song time. But we never do. All you and daddy ever do is press your phones and work. Why go out to nature if you are only going to work?" Anna asked and her siblings nodded in agreement.

"We would prefer to be at home rather than go out to camp with you both. We always have more fun here at home than over there at camp. Camp is always so boring because you both never want to do anything but work. It is the five of us that always play together," this came from Elisa.

Their parents were surprised. They had never realized what they always did. The children stood up and said together, at the same time,

"May we be excused?"

"Yes, you can go," their parents said.

When the children left, the parents looked at each other sadly. They only wanted their children to have fun. They had had no idea that the children hated the camping trips. They were right. They worked a lot, even during camping when it should be fun time for the family.

"We have to do something about it. We have to spend time with them and help them have fun during camping," their father said.

Their mother nodded, "Yes, we have to make sure the children love camping and have fun. Now, what do we do?"

Their parents tapped their chins as they thought about how they could make it up to their children. Then, a light bulb went on in their mother's head and she exclaimed,

"I know what we have to do! We are going to give our children the best camping trip they have ever had! Here is what we have to do."

She leaned close to her husband and whispered and whispered and whispered.

And so, the next day, their large car was driving up the road to the park where they were going to go camping. In the back of the car, the children were frowning again. Their parents had refused to listen to them and now, they were heading out to yet another boring camping trip. Or so, they thought.

When they got to their camping site, as always, they set up their tents and then, the kitchen. The five children were about to head into the tent to read the books they brought along when their parents called out to them.

"Where are you going to?"

"To read, what else? While you both are working, we will be reading together. It is what we always do," Anna answered for her and her siblings.

"Well, things are about to change because your father and I have activities planned out for the family. So, there's no time to read alone or to work.

We are just going to have fun as a family," their mother told them.

"What? Do you really mean that?" Becca asked.

"I don't believe. It's too good to be true," Devon said and Elisa nodded in agreement with him.

"We listened to you kids and I promise that we are going to have loads of fun."

"Hmm... Seeing is believing," Anna said, "What do you have planned for us?"

"First hiking!"

"But, we didn't bring boots and..." the children started protesting.

"We've got that taken care of," their parents grinned as they presented the children with new boots.

"Let's go!"

Laughing the family headed to the hiking trails. Before they went up the trails, their parents also gave them bird watching books. They headed up the trails pointing out the birds that they saw.

"Shall we have a scavenger hunt?" their father asked when they stopped to rest.

"Yes! Yes! Yes!" the children exclaimed immediately.

They divided into groups of three with Anna, Chad and Elisa in one group and Becca, Devon and their father were in another group. Their mother was the game runner.

"Let the games begin!" Their mother declared.

Laughing, they all parted ways. It was an alphabetical scavenger hunt and they had to find an ant, a bee, a creek, dew, an evergreen tree, a flower, grass, a hole, an insect, a jug, a knot, leaves,

a mound of dirt, a nest, an oak tree, a pine cone, a quick animal, a river, a stone, a tree stump, an umbrella, a view, a walking stick, an 'X' on a map, a 'Y' shaped stick and a zip. All they had to do was take pictures of them and they planned to make a photo album when they were done!

They ran up and down the trail and around the camp too, trying to best each other. A few hours later, Anna's team had found all the items on the list first.

The tired but excited family returned to the camp.

"Let's have a shower and eat dinner. What do we think?" their dad asked.

"Yes! Yes! Yes!" they all shouted in unison.

The family sat down to eat dinner after which, the children cleaned up. As they cleaned the camp, they sang,

Wash the plates, wash the plates,

After eating, after eating,

Wash with soap and water,

Wash with soap and water,

The plates are clean, they're ready to be dried.

Wipe the table, Wipe the table,

After eating, after eating,

Wipe with soap and water,

Wipe with soap and water,

The table is clean, flies will stay away!

Once they were done with the chores, their parents presented a pack of cards and board games.

"Let's play!!"

"I win!!" Chad shouted at the end of the game.

Now that the game was over, the family settled down to build a fire. They sat around the campfire, staring up at the stars. The stars were sparkling and beautiful and Elisa started singing:

Twinkle, twinkle, little star,

How I wonder what you are,

Up above the world so high,

Like a diamond in the sky,

Twinkle, twinkle, little star,

How I wonder what you are...

Slowly, they all joined in and sang under the night sky, staring up at the stars.

Their father stepped away and he returned with a guitar. As soon as the children saw him, they cheered.

"Play a song for us, daddy!"

"Sure, I will my little ones." Their father winked.

Starry, starry, starry night...

Starry night...

Starry night..

Starry, starry, starry night,

It's a starry night, a starry night...

Sitting, sitting, by the campfire...

Under this starry night, it's a starry night...

The company is so perfect...

Under this starry night, starry night...

Starry, starry, starry night...

Starry night...

Starry night...

They all hummed along with the guitar as their father sang for them. They danced along slowly, enjoying the cold night air, the heat from the campfire and the marshmallows they were toasting. It was a fun night under the starry night.

At midnight, the fire was doused and they all retreated into the large tent.

"So did you have fun today kids? Your mother and I have another fun day planned out for us tomorrow."

"Yes, daddy! We had lots of fun!" they said as they snuggled in their respective sleeping bags.

"We are sorry we have been so busy, kids. We promise that we will always spend time with you. This camping trip is just the start of many fun activities we will do together as a family," their mother told them and she hugged Elisa, sleeping bag and all. "We love you!"

"We love you too!"

"Please sing us to sleep, daddy..."

"With pleasure.."

Good night, sleep tight...

Until tomorrow, when I'll see you again...

Good night, my dears....

Until tomorrow, when I'll see you again...

Sweet dreams, good dreams,

Have them and sleep well,

Good night, my dears,

Until tomorrow, when I'll see you again...

Printed in Great Britain
by Amazon

76028535R00066